# How the Camel got his Hump

Retold by Anna Milbourne

Illustrated by John Joven

Reading consultant: Alison Kelly

Long ago, Camel didn't have a hump.

This story tells how
he got one.

When the world was new, there was lots of work to do.

But grumpy Camel
didn't want to work.

He wanted to eat.

“Please help me bring sticks,” said Dog.

"Humph!" said
grumpy Camel.

"Please help me carry branches," said Horse.

"Humph!" said grumpy Camel.

"Please help me pull the cart," said Ox.

“Humph!” said grumpy Camel.

Man said, “If Camel won’t help, you must all work harder.”

“You need to work,”
the Genie told Camel.

Humph!

"Please make Camel work!" the animals begged.

The animals were cross.

Suddenly a magic Genie appeared.

“Last chance,” said the Genie.

So the Genie did some magic...

"What's that?" wailed Camel.

"Your humph!" the Genie laughed.

"The hump stores food," explained the Genie.

"Now you can work
without stopping
for lunch."

Since then, Camel has always worked hard.

But he is still very,
very grumpy!

# PUZZLES

## Puzzle 1

Spot five differences between the two pictures.

## Puzzle 2

Put the pictures in order.

A

A Genie
gave Camel
a hump.

B

Now Camel
works hard.

C

Grumpy Camel
wouldn't work.

# Puzzle 3

## Choose the right speech bubble for each picture.

3
Please help me pull the cart.
Please help me find the cart.
4
Yes, I'll help you!
Humph!

# Answers to puzzles

## Puzzle 1

## Puzzle 2

1C Grumpy Camel wouldn't work.

2A A Genie gave Camel a hump.

3B Now Camel works hard.

## Puzzle 3

1

Please help me bring sticks.

2

Please help me carry branches.

3

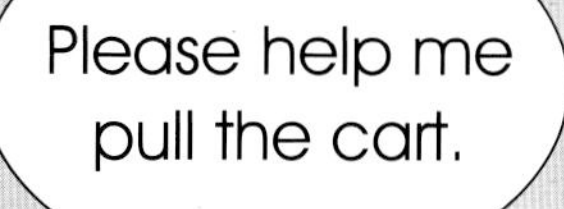


4

Humph!

# About the story

This story is from the book *Just So Stories* by Rudyard Kipling, which tells how animals came to be the way they are.

Designed by Laura Nelson Norris
Series designer: Russell Punter
Series editor: Lesley Sims

First published in 2017 by Usborne Publishing Ltd., Usborne House, 83-85 Saffron Hill, London EC1N 8RT, England. www.usborne.com